S0-BEZ-501

PUFFIN BOOKS
WISHA WOZZARITER

Payal Kapadia studied English Literature at St Xavier's College, Bombay, and Journalism at Northwestern University in Chicago. She has worked with *Outlook* in Bombay and *The Japan Times* in Tokyo.

She now lives in Bombay with her husband Kunal Bajaj, two daughters Keya and Nyla, and their three imaginary friends: Klixa, Pallading and Kiki. Her first book *Colonel Hathi Loses His Brigade* was published by Disney in 2011.

Wisha Wozzariter

Payal Kapadia

Illustrated by Roger Dahl

PUFFIN BOOKS

PUFFIN BOOKS

Published by the Penguin Group

Penguin Books India Pvt. Ltd, 7th Floor, Infinity Tower C, DLF Cyber City, Gurgaon 122 002, Haryana, India

Penguin Group (USA) Inc., 375 Hudson Street, New York, New York 10014, USA

Penguin Group (Canada), 90 Eglinton Avenue East, Suite 700, Toronto, Ontario, M4P 2Y3, Canada

Penguin Books Ltd, 80 Strand, London WC2R 0RL, England

Penguin Ireland, 25 St Stephen's Green, Dublin 2, Ireland (a division of Penguin Books Ltd)

Penguin Group (Australia), 707 Collins Street, Melbourne, Victoria 3008, Australia

Penguin Group (NZ), 67 Apollo Drive, Rosedale, Auckland 0632, New Zealand

Penguin Books (South Africa) (Pty) Ltd, Block D, Rosebank Office Park, 181 Jan Smuts Avenue, Parktown North, Johannesburg 2193, South Africa

Penguin Books Ltd, Registered Offices: 80 Strand, London WC2R 0RL, England

First published in Puffin by Penguin Books India 2012

Text copyright © Payal Kapadia 2012
Illustrations copyright © Roger Dahl 2012

All rights reserved

10 9 8 7 6 5 4 3 2

Reprinted in 2014

ISBN 9780143332114

Typeset in Sabon MT by Eleven Arts, Keshav Puram, New Delhi
Printed at Repro India Ltd., Navi Mumbai

This book is sold subject to the condition that it shall not, by way of trade or otherwise, be lent, resold, hired out, or otherwise circulated without the publisher's prior written consent in any form of binding or cover other than that in which it is published and without a similar condition including this condition being imposed on the subsequent purchaser and without limiting the rights under copyright reserved above, no part of this publication may be reproduced, stored in or introduced into a retrieval system, or transmitted in any form or by any means (electronic, mechanical, photocopying, recording or otherwise), without the prior written permission of both the copyright owner and the above-mentioned publisher of this book.

A PENGUIN RANDOM HOUSE COMPANY

To my parents Rohit and Sandhya, who first made me feel like a writer, my husband Kunal, who pays the price for being married to one, and my daughters Keya and Nyla, who won't have dinner without a story.

—Payal Kapadia

For my parents, Reuben and Madeline, and sisters, Marilyn and Dolly, who always encouraged me to colour outside the lines.

—Roger Dahl

Contents

Contents

Acknowledgements

I wrote the first half of *Wisha Wozzariter* eight years ago. I would have still been wishing I were a writer if it hadn't been for my editor at Penguin, Sohini Mitra, who popped up one fine day, Bookworm-like, to ask the all-important question: 'Why don't you?'

Thank you, Sohini, for taking me on an adventure-filled journey from moth-eaten manuscript to published book.

This also goes out to Roger, my Prufrock, my fellow-explorer, for whom no idea was ever too abstract or too over the top to draw. I cannot thank you enough, Roger, for lifting my book and transforming it.

Thank you, Bhavi Mehta, for tolerating our wild ideas and for tempering them with all your knowledge about how the publishing world really works.

And thanks to Puffin for putting my story out for the world to see. I only hope my publishers are sitting on the last page now, like the Bookworm, looking mighty pleased.

Wisha

Wisha Wozzariter loved reading. She read before school and after school. She read before lunch and after lunch. She read before dinner and after dinner. She would have read all day and all night if she could.

Wisha hated bad books, but she hated one thing even more: good ones. Good books always left her feeling she could do better if she were to write a book of her own. She'd put down a good book, sighing, 'Now that's a book I could have written.'

On her tenth birthday, Wisha read Roald Dahl's *Charlie and the Chocolate Factory*. She hated it more than anything. There was no reason something this good should not have been written by her. She got to the last word on the last page, then sighed, 'Now that's a book I could have written!'

'Why don't you?' said a green little worm, popping his head out of page no. 64.

'Who are you?' asked Wisha, startled.

'Why, a Bookworm, who else?' said the worm, sounding surprised. 'I've heard you say the same thing after every good book. So why don't you?'

'Why don't I—what?' said Wisha.

'Write a book, write a book,' said the Bookworm in a sing-song voice, wriggling his way out on to the cover.

'I wish I was a writer,' sighed Wisha.

'Well, you are Wisha Wozzariter,' said the Bookworm.

'So I am! But I don't quite know where to begin.'

'At the beginning, of course,' said the Bookworm, rolling his eyes. 'Got some time?'

'Yee-es. Why, what do you suggest?' asked Wisha.

'A trip to the Marketplace of Ideas,' said the Bookworm. 'My treat.'

Wisha jumped up. 'Sounds more exciting than wishing all day! How do we get there?'

'Close your eyes and hold my hand tight,' said the Bookworm. 'We're catching the Thought Express.'

'When does it come in?' asked Wisha.

'Don't know. Are your thoughts always on time?'

'Not really.'

'Well, then, we might have a little wait ahead of us,' said the Bookworm. 'It would help if you were to say your name to yourself a few times.'

So Wisha closed her eyes and said, 'Wisha Wozzariter, Wisha Wozzariter, Wisha Wozzariter.'

The Thought Express was a little slow and a little late, but it came in, sure enough. And when it left for the Marketplace of Ideas, Wisha and the Bookworm were on it.

*

The Marketplace of Ideas

'Looking for ideas?' asked a scrawny young fellow in a loose brown coat, with more pockets than it had buttons on it. 'Big ones? Small ones? I specialize in small ones.'

Wisha stared at him in disbelief, and then all around her in bewilderment. The marketplace was a complete mess. She did not think there was a clear idea to be found here. Some vendors stood outside their stalls, on tall stools, shouting out their wares. Others, like the skinny specialist of small ideas standing before her, mingled with the crowd. Buyers jostled with sellers.

'New ideas for old! New ideas for old!' cried a woman dragging a bag full of polishing rags behind her. 'I repair old ideas. I shine old ideas. I recycle old ideas. Nothing is so old it cannot be made new.'

Pickup vans filled with ideas blared their horns

impatiently. A garbage-collection truck trundled along. 'Don't litter the roads with your tired, old ideas. Deposit them here!' it said on the side of it.

At one stall, a bearded artist kept picking up bottle after bottle of ideas, uncorking the lid and sniffing at the mouth. 'Just doesn't smell like a masterpiece,' he grumbled.

A handcart stacked with cages of ideas tried to make an uncertain path through all the pell-mell. It tipped over, the cages skittering across the pavement and one cage door flying open. Out staggered a baby idea, squawking like a chicken before flapping its wings and taking flight.

A red-haired man immediately jumped off the handcart, holding his head and running behind the baby idea. He tried to clutch at its legs, but it was too high up in the air already. 'My idea, my idea!' he cried, almost hurtling into Wisha. 'It's escaped me.'

'Get a grip,' droned a salesgirl standing outside the IdeaMart. 'We're open 24×7,' she said, as if by rote. 'We never run out of ideas. Lost an idea? Get another here.'

She was not the only one selling ideas. Neon advertisements hung overhead. A plane made its arc across the sky, leaving a jet trail behind that read: For ideas that really take off, call 1-800-IDEASHOP.

Wisha was so busy looking up at the sky, she didn't see the pail of water being sloshed out on the street. Before she knew it, she was dripping wet. 'Get out of the way!' said a boy crossly, the empty pail still clanging in his hand. The other boys gathered around him, giggling. 'Don't you know better than to wander down New Idea Street, looking up at the sky?'

The Bookworm nudged Wisha along before she could retort. 'They're clearing up the old ideas here to make place for new ones,' he said. 'Better not to fight them unless you want a bucket of old ideas to be emptied on your head!'

Wisha moved ahead, reluctantly. At the end of the road, she could now see what appeared to be the gloomiest building she had ever set her eyes upon. Dark spires reached up to the sky; the black stone walls had no windows; and in front, huge iron gates stood locked, with four guards in front of them.

'Is this a prison of some sort?' she asked the Bookworm.

'It is,' he nodded nervously before ushering her past it. 'Bad ideas are kept in custody here. Like Slavery, for example. That has been one of our worst

offenders. Keeps trying to escape under the guise of Racism.'

'You mean Slavery is serving time here?'

'Yes, and so would War if we could have our way,' said the Bookworm. 'Trouble is, the world isn't ready to get rid of some bad ideas.'

This was all too much for Wisha to take in at one time. 'Where are we?' she asked finally, in total disbelief. 'You mean to say, every idea in the world is found here? Sold here?'

'Not sold,' said the Bookworm, shaking his head firmly. 'Exchanged. You must give them one idea in exchange for another.'

'Am I going to get *my* ideas here?'

'You could—but I'm taking you to a better place. Come along, we better hurry or else the best ideas will be gone.'

With that, the Bookworm pushed Wisha down New Idea Street, past Old Idea Souk and over the Bridge of Ideas to the biggest event of the marketplace.

'This is where the best ideas are exchanged,' he whispered to Wisha as they stepped in.

*

The Grand Idea Auction

'Anyone for an idea to make pots of money?' bellowed the auctioneer.

Most of the people in the audience raised their hands. Wisha and the Bookworm didn't.

'A hundred ideas in exchange is the starting price here,' said the auctioneer. 'Not a bad price for something that will make you rich.'

'Two hundred, I say,' said an old lady with short, wispy hair, sitting in the back.

'Three,' immediately followed a bespectacled man seated next to Wisha.

'Four,' countered a little girl seated next to her mother.

And so it went, one price beating the next, till that money-making idea was sold—for 1,000 smaller ideas!—to the old lady.

The next item on sale was an idea to get famous.

Once again, almost everyone was bidding, except Wisha and the Bookworm.

'How about this? An idea to change the world!' shouted the auctioneer. Wisha shot up her hand, but the Bookworm caught it in time, forcing it back down.

'Didn't I tell you to wait?' he said.

'But all we've done is wait,' she said, impatient now. 'This sounds like a good idea to me.'

'It is—for someone who wants to change the world. You said you wanted to write, didn't you?'

This made no sense to Wisha. 'Of course I do,' she said. 'But don't writers change the world?'

'They might,' said the Bookworm. 'But they don't write to change the world, any more than they do to make pots of money or to get famous. This idea is of no use to you.'

Wisha waited as idea after idea fell under the hammer. An idea to save the environment went for 3,000 smaller ideas; another idea to move the hearts of men went for 2,000. Then it came, the idea the Bookworm had been waiting for.

'Are there any takers for this one?' said the auctioneer, looking doubtful as his surly assistant held up what looked like a deflated red balloon.

'It was once sold to Lewis Carroll, who held on to it for years. But our last buyer returned it to us, saying it doesn't work any more.'

'Ladies and gentleman,' he said. 'May I present the Imagination Balloon?'

There was silence in the audience.

'Umm . . . It *does* have antique value,' ventured the auctioneer, but not one of them raised their hands.

'Now!' said the Bookworm. 'Tell him you'll have it.'

Wisha shot her hand straight up. 'Me! I'll have it!'

Wisha should not have looked so eager.

A sly look spread across the auctioneer's face. Stroking his curly moustache, he said, 'And what will you give me in return?'

'I always have plenty of ideas, how many do you need?' Wisha asked.

'Hmmm,' said the auctioneer. 'Not ideas, we have enough of those by now. Tell you what, give me a bottle of Inspiration.'

Wisha tried to reply, but the Bookworm cut her short. 'Come now, a bottle is too much to ask of a first-time writer, you know that! We'll give you half a bottle, or you can find yourself another buyer.'

The auctioneer leaned back, narrowing his eyes. 'You? Still after the Imagination Balloon when it did precious little for that fellow you brought with you the last time?'

Saying that, he brought the hammer down with a resounding thud. 'It's yours. The Imagination Balloon is yours for half a bottle of Inspiration, to be delivered to us by the end of this year.'

So that was how Wisha Wozzariter took her Imagination home with her, although there was no instruction booklet on how to use it.

*

The Imagination Balloon

'It doesn't work!' cried Wisha in dismay for the umpteenth time. Try as she might, she could not inflate the Imagination Balloon. As for Bookworm, he had disappeared into one of the books on the shelf and hadn't come out in days.

Wisha picked up Harper Lee's *To Kill a Mockingbird* and started reading. Only midway, she sighed, 'I wish I was a writer. I could do better than this.'

'Why don't you?' said the Bookworm, sticking his head out of page 11.

'Well, there you are!' said Wisha. 'What do you mean, leaving me all alone like that with this red balloon?'

'You're not alone,' said the Bookworm. 'Don't you have yourself to keep you company?'

Saying that, he handed Wisha a sheet of black paper with a white door drawn in it. It said 'SOLITUDE ONLY—OTHERS KEEP OUT!'

'What's this?' Wisha began to ask, but the Bookworm was already gone.

Wisha turned the sheet of paper over. It had the door drawn on both sides, the door-knob sticking out of the page like a walnut. She closed her fingers around the knob and opened the door.

She stuck her head in, although it was a tight squeeze. She couldn't see a thing. It felt cramped. She hesitated—it didn't make any sense. Nothing did. Then, she stepped inside, pulling the balloon into the room with her. The room seemed to expand to make space for her and the balloon. And then the door swung shut.

Inside, it was dark and silent, except for the sound of Wisha's thoughts, whooshing and whishing through the air like paper rockets. She put the balloon to her lips and started blowing.

It was hard going. At first, nothing happened. Then something clattered into the balloon. An orange bicycle.

'Where did that come from? From inside me?' wondered Wisha.

Next came the clinking sound of a bunch of metal keys. Wisha could see them through the skin of the balloon.

Then, nothing. She blew till she was blue in the face, but the balloon wouldn't get any bigger.

Pulling the door open, the Bookworm stuck his head in. 'Any luck yet? What's this?'

Wisha showed him the bicycle and the metal keys, trapped inside the balloon.

'Your Imagination isn't throwing up too much,' observed the Bookworm. 'Perhaps you haven't been keeping your eyes open.'

'It's not as though I walk about with my eyes shut, you know,' retorted Wisha, growing a little weary of the Bookworm's remarks.

'Not true,' said the Bookworm, whipping out a pair of silver spectacles. 'You will be surprised to know that most people master the art of sleepwalking very early in life. Now, these are Observation Glasses. Put them on.'

'I can see quite well, thank you,' said Wisha, a little offended.

'Can you?' said the Bookworm. 'Then why don't you have enough in your Imagination to fill up this balloon?'

Wisha decided not to answer that question. 'What's going to happen when I wear these?' she asked impatiently.

'What's going to happen?' said the Bookworm, repeating her question. 'What's going to happen, Wisha Wozzariter, is that you'll find things you've seen and not noticed. Things you've heard but not listened to. Touched but not felt. Said but not meant. Smelt but not experienced. Take all those things, my dear Wisha, and blow them into your balloon. Just do it! I'll be back.'

*

What Wisha Saw

When she was all alone in the darkness again, Wisha put on her spectacles. It took a few moments for her senses to adjust to the feeling that everything around her was magnified. She could see the darkness of the room she was standing in; yes, actually *see* the darkness and its thick velvetiness.

All sorts of sounds came to her ears from beyond the room, each sound with its own texture: the rough, ringing sound of a squirrel's tail against the bark of a tree; the whisper of leaves rustling on the almond tree outside her home; the thwack of a cricket bat connecting with a ball as the boys played their evening matches; the deep-throated rumble of monsoon clouds gearing up to shed their rain.

Other sounds, too, more frightening ones. The shrillness of brakes screaming for mercy before her neighbour's car dashed into a tree last year; the sparrows crying after the crow stole their eggs, and so on.

Wisha drew a sharp inward breath. With it came the smell, clean like soap, of the earth after the rain—and that feeling of running in and out of the rain, just in time, to the smell of dinner cooking.

Her fingers were tingling now, as if all ten of them were recalling their own memories: of the windowpanes quivering like piano wires against the wind; the stickiness of a torn flower petal; the furry nothingness of a butterfly's wing; the rough promise of a page she had never read before.

There was a sigh building up inside her now, and that sigh was turning into a song, and that song was turning into a cry; and now she was crying, big tears rolling down her face, smearing their wetness upon her cheeks and dropping down uncertainly around her mouth.

Hands trembling, Wisha Wozzariter brought the balloon to her lips and she blew; she blew her entire being into that balloon. Everything she had seen but not noticed; heard but not listened to; touched but not felt; meant but not said; smelt but not experienced went rushing into that balloon. It grew larger—and larger—and larger—till it was almost bursting open from the life inside it.

When the Bookworm popped his head in, he found Wisha floating in her Solitude Room, light as a feather, astride a big red balloon.

Hero Zero

'How do I explain what happened to me in that room?' asked Wisha of the Bookworm. 'I felt . . . I felt . . .'

'Inspired!' completed the Bookworm. He was curled up around a clear-blue bottle. A few round drops of something gold and glistening clung to the inside of it.

'That's your Inspiration, Wisha Wozzariter,' said the Bookworm. 'You were inspired in that room and when you're inspired enough to write your book, this bottle will be full. So full that you'll be able to spare a half-bottle for that auctioneer, you'll see.'

Having said that, the Bookworm slid off the bottle and into page 101 of *The Adventures of Tom Sawyer*. Wisha picked up her pen and as if she had always known what to do next, dipped it into the bottle of Inspiration and started writing.

But hardly had she written a line or two when she realized that she had imagined everything except a hero. Roald Dahl had Charlie, Lewis Carroll had Alice; Wisha Wozzariter had given her readers no one to love or hate.

'Where's Bookworm when I need him?' she said, flipping through the pages of *The Adventures of Tom Sawyer*. There was no sight of him. Wisha searched for another hour but the Bookworm did not return. She sat back, tired, and stared at the Inspiration bottle, at her Imagination Balloon, at the white door with its walnut knob leading to the Solitude Room—and thought of a way out.

Or a way in? Yes, that was it, thought Wisha, as she reached for the door to Solitude and opened it again. She stepped in and allowed the darkness to settle like fine dust around her shoulders. In the silence, she heard the whistle of a train coming in. This time, it was on schedule.

'Stand aside for the Thought Express,' whispered a voice in the darkness. 'Next stop, Bargain Bazaar. Get on—or keep waiting. What will it be?'

Wisha couldn't decide. Her stomach was knotting up inside her. This time, there was no Bookworm for company; she was all on her own. She felt the wheels of the train start to move again. There was no time for second thoughts.

'I'm coming!' she cried, jumping on. As her thoughts hurtled her on to who knows where, her hands closed around something. It was a discount ticket of some sort. It said:

Dear First-Time Writer,
This ticket entitles you to 50% off at the Thrift Shop, the one-stop shop for Cheap Characters and Second-hand Heroes.

The Superhero Salon

The Thought Express took Wisha to the Bargain Bazaar—well, almost. Most of the passengers wanted to get off at the Superhero Salon so that's where the train stopped.

'Sorry about that,' whispered a voice into Wisha's ear. 'If you don't get what you're looking for here, the Bargain Bazaar isn't too far off.'

Wisha alighted from the train, dazzled. The floor beneath her feet was paved with coins. All around her, white marble pillars rose up to a stained-glass roof, gleaming. Gold elevators swished up and down between the pillars as soft music streamed into the sunlit building. Fountains of silver water sprang up into the air.

'May I help you?' said a lady, dressed immaculately in black. Her smile seemed to rip apart her face.

'I'm a little lost,' said Wisha. 'Where am I?'

The lady's smile flickered like the flame of a dying candle, her lips thinning. 'We-ell, if you don't know where you are, perhaps you shouldn't be here, hmmm?'

'I came in on the Thought Express,' said Wisha by way of explanation.

'I'll have a word with that engine driver later,' said the lady, not looking pleased. 'We can't have anyone and everyone turning up here just because the Thought took hold of them.'

'Please,' said Wisha. 'I'm here to find a Hero. I can pay.'

'Suit yourself, take a look around then,' said the lady, and she was gone.

There was nothing but the cash desks on the ground floor, so Wisha took the elevator up. 'Floor One—Apparel,' said the pretty elevator-girl, bowing. 'This is where the heroes get their outfits,' she said. 'Unless you prefer to check out Floor Two first, that'll give you an idea how they look once they have their hair and make-up done.'

'No, thanks,' said Wisha, bewildered. 'I'll just get off here.'

No one spared a glance her way as she walked around Floor One. All the sales staff was busy pandering to rich customers.

'I'd like my hero dapper like James Bond,' said a white-haired woman who looked like a schoolteacher. 'No, not that suit, the other one.'

'I want mine nice and naughty—like Artemis Fowl,' giggled her friend, thin as a reed and tall. The hero standing before her looked too nice to be naughty. His face fell as the sales staff led him away.

A loud wail went up from the little girl at the other end of the floor. 'Mommeee, she's not pwetty enuff!' she said, stamping her foot upon the ground. 'I want a real fairy, a real fairy!'

'Darling,' said the little girl's mother. 'She is a real fairy. We'll give her golden hair and some sparkly make-up and she'll look better than a real one.'

The little girl was inconsolable and started howling in the most hideous fashion. The mother took her by the hand and tucked the fairy under one arm.

'Take us to the Make-Up Section,' she said imperiously to the saleslady. The fairy didn't look too happy being carried away like that. Her wand fell on the floor as they left, but they didn't stop to pick it up.

'Uh, excuse me,' said Wisha, stopping a sales clerk. 'I'd like a hero, too.'

'What would you like, madam?' said the clerk, his

smile reminding Wisha of the lady she had met on the Ground Floor.

'I'd like a girl-hero,' said Wisha. 'She must be brave and strong and feisty.'

She quickly added, 'Oh, and awfully clever, too!'

'You're asking for a lot,' said the sales clerk. 'It'll cost you.'

'I can pay,' said Wisha proudly. Hadn't she bought the Imagination Balloon for half a bottle of Inspiration?

'Hey, Marcy, get a load of this,' said the sales clerk, calling across the room to his colleague. 'She says she can pay.'

Hoots of laughter emanated from the general direction of Marcy, wherever she was. Wisha squirmed in discomfort.

'What's so funny?' she asked the clerk.

'Ma'am, we don't accept payment here. Only Frequent Shopper's Cards. Do you have one?'

Wisha shook her head. 'How can I get one?' she asked him.

He tittered. 'By shopping here frequently, of course.'

'But I can't shop here without a card, can I?' asked Wisha, puzzled.

'Of course you can't,' said the clerk. He was enjoying this.

'This doesn't make sense,' protested Wisha. 'You won't let me shop here because I don't have a card! But I don't have a card because you won't let me shop here!'

'Now, ma'am,' said the clerk, dropping his voice so low it was almost inaudible. 'Let's not create a scene. Why don't we resolve this outside?'

It was a question, but the clerk didn't wait for Wisha's reply. He scooped her up by her waist and tucked her under his arm like bothersome baggage, then marched her past the elevator, down the winding stairs, and out the door of the Superhero Salon.

'You're out of your league here,' he hissed as he put her down hard. 'Try the Bargain Bazaar.'

*

The Bargain Bazaar

The smooth pavement outside the Superhero Salon quickly gave way to a dirt-road pockmarked with potholes. Trails of slush marked the path to the Bargain Bazaar. Rusted poles propped up the tattered tarpaulin roof, and they were dripping with grease. The grey roof sagged at the corners, and through a large tear in the middle, you could see the sky, also grey.

Wisha coughed as a cloud of dust materialized in front of her. A stoutly built fellow in a black velveteen coat was dusting the shelves of his shop with a cloth that looked too dirty to clean anything.

'Want a look at our second-hand wares, miss?' he rasped, his voice sounding like he had stones in his throat.

Before Wisha could show any interest, he rattled on. 'They're a little worse for wear, our heroes, but that's only because they've been used before.'

His eyes glinted like a knife-edge catching the light. 'And we charge a little more for heroes that well-known writers once used. Dickens' heroes turned up the other day, a little roughed up, but we're getting them in order, as we speak.'

He clapped his hands twice. 'We've got a customer here!'

'No, you don't,' said Wisha. 'I'd like to look around the bazaar, if you don't mind.'

The man stepped in front of her. Up close, he towered over her. 'What's to look at, little girl? You think you'll get better elsewhere?'

Wisha tried to move past him. 'No, no, nothing like that,' she hastened to say. 'It's just that I have this coupon for the Thrift Shop and I'd like to go there first.'

The man clutched at her T-shirt. 'The Thrift Shop? Did you say the Thrift Shop? It burned down ten years ago. Give me that!'

His hand shot out, trying to snatch the coupon from her. Wisha screamed at the sudden shock of it all. He had his hands on the coupon now and he was tugging at it. She felt it beginning to rip apart. In horror, both she and the man let go of it.

A rogue wind whistled through the bazaar,

whipping the coupon up and sending it fluttering across. Wisha stared after it in dismay, then pushed past the man and raced behind it. By the time she caught up with it, she was at the end of the bazaar, panting for breath. The ticket fell to the ground, as if exhausted. There was a nasty tear running through it, but it was still in one piece. Wisha stooped down to pick it up, but another pair of hands beat her to it.

'You'll want to show this to me,' said a cheerful voice. A short fellow on tiny legs, sweating profusely, stood in front of her, waving the ticket in her face.

'The Thrift Shop might be gone, but I'm the owner Mr Frugal and I'm still here,' he said.

Wisha lunged for the ticket, but he stopped her. 'You're not the first person who seems to want this ticket. Give it back,' she said. She couldn't help staring at Mr Frugal, drenched in his own perspiration.

'Ah, so I see that you've met Sikes, have you?' said Mr Frugal. 'He would do anything for that ticket, Miss Wozzariter, and if I were you, I'd guard it closely.'

Seeing her start at the mention of her name, he said, 'Yes, of course, I've been expecting you. You don't think you got this ticket just by Chance, do you? Never ever underestimate the play of Destiny in a writer's fortunes.'

'So I was *meant* to come here,' said Wisha slowly. 'You must have a hero for me then.'

'I do,' said Mr Frugal. 'I had her somewhere,' he said, looking all about him. 'Now where is she?'

He took off his shoe and shook it out. A grey mouse fell out. A grey mouse that was rapidly turning purple. *Purple!*

'Here she is!' said Mr Frugal.

'A mouse?' cried Wisha in disbelief. 'A mouse! And why did she just turn purple before my eyes?'

'Er, this mouse has a rather strange—or shall we say special—quality . . .' said Mr Frugal, looking a little embarrassed.

Wisha said nothing. In her mind, she was trying to come to terms with the idea of a hero many sizes smaller than she had imagined her to be, and of the wrong colour.

'She turns purple when she's . . .' and here, Mr Frugal paused to clear his throat. It was easy to see that he was uncomfortable about this.

'. . . scared,' he said finally. 'She turns purple when she's scared.'

The mouse was hiding under Mr Frugal's collar,

trembling with fright. At these last words from Mr Frugal, she jumped.

Mr Frugal dropped his voice to a whisper. Leaning in close, he told Wisha, 'She's even scared of being scared.'

'Is this what you call a hero?' cried Wisha.

'Well, I don't have to call her a hero,' replied Mr Frugal. 'You do.'

He smiled and added: 'If you want to, that is.'

Then laughing a deep-throated laugh at Wisha's dismay, he continued: 'Still, it doesn't get better these days, you know. Even heroes aren't what they used to be. You'll just have to make the most of her.'

Gently, he picked the mouse off his shoulder and handed her to Wisha.

'She's a good one,' said Mr Frugal. 'And she's all I have left. You can take her for free; I have no place to keep her.'

The purple mouse twitched her whiskers as Wisha peered at her. Then she scampered up Wisha's leg and into the folds of her shorts. She sat there, quivering.

It would take a lot of work to make a hero out of her, thought Wisha.

'I guess I should be thankful, Mr Frugal,' she said finally. 'I'd better go.'

She walked away, back through the Bargain Bazaar and up the slushy streets.

'Miss Wozzariter, wait up!' shouted Mr Frugal, running up behind her. 'I'll walk you to the station. You won't be able to catch the Thought Express from the Superhero Salon any more.'

Mr Frugal waited with Wisha and her purple mouse till the train came in. And when it did, he thrust the torn discount ticket back into her hand. 'You forgot your ticket, Miss Wozzariter,' he shouted as the train pulled out of the station. 'Don't let it out of your sight again. There's a Golden Scratch Card behind it, you see!'

Wisha turned the ticket over and stared at the rectangular patch of gold on the back. 'It's for Luck!' she heard Mr Frugal saying, his voice sounding so much farther away now. 'A writer can be the best writer in the world, but without a stroke of Luck, he'll go nowhere.'

*

Meeting Prufrock

The Solitude Room was no place for a purple mouse. She scurried up Wisha's leg and sniffed nervously around her feet as Wisha blew into her Imagination Balloon.

There was a low hiss as *Pumpernickel* slipped into the balloon.

Now that's a good name for my purple mouse, thought Wisha, but where did it come from?

She took a deep breath and started blowing the balloon again. *Selinda* came next.

Selinda? Not good enough for a heroine, thought Wisha, but I'm not discarding it just yet.

And so it went, as name after possible name suggested itself until the balloon was beginning to look uncomfortably full and Wisha herself was getting a little purple in the face from blowing that hard.

The mouse brushed against her ankles. Putting the balloon aside, Wisha bent down and scooped her up.

'Now what am I going to call you?' she mused aloud.

'Are you asking me my name?' said the purple mouse in a painfully shy voice.

'You have a name already?' exclaimed Wisha in disbelief. 'Well, then, yes!'

'It's Prufrock,' said the mouse. 'I'm touched that you thought to ask.'

'Prufrock . . .' said Wisha. 'That's better than anything I could have thought of!'

'Names are great that way,' said Prufrock. 'Either a name grows to suit its wearer, or the wearer grows to suit his name. I don't know what came first, my name or me, but yes, we go together.'

Wisha had so many questions for Prufrock: What was it like being a mouse? What was it like being a purple mouse? Was she the only purple mouse in the world?

At first, Prufrock was too scared to say much. It didn't help that just as Prufrock was beginning to settle down, the Bookworm stuck his head in.

'Getting to know your character, Wisha?' he

shouted. I can imagine that it would be hard to write about someone you don't know.'

The Bookworm's sudden appearance made Prufrock turn bright purple and run for cover inside Wisha's sleeve.

It took plenty of gentle coaxing from Wisha for Prufrock to come out of her hiding place, but once the Bookworm had gone, she did.

'I wish I weren't so scared,' said Prufrock. 'But I don't think I've ever been anything but.'

*

Once upon a time, Prufrock had been anything but scared. When she was a baby, she was always wandering away on her own, out of her mother's sight. The house they lived in belonged to an artist who hated mice. He had set many traps for them, but Prufrock's mother had always been too clever to get caught. She worried for Prufrock, but Prufrock had never known fear.

One day, Prufrock crept under a table when her mother wasn't looking. She remembered it clearly: there were two crumbs of bread and the tiniest morsel of cheese under that table. *Cheese!* Prufrock went closer and sniffed at the cheese. Just then, her mother spotted her.

'Mousetrap, Prufrock!' she cried. 'Run!'

Terrified, Prufrock bolted out from under the table and straight into a pair of human legs.

'A mouse!' boomed a loud human voice. It was the artist!

'Somebody, get the broom!' he shouted.

In a trice, the long end of a wooden broom was thumping the floor around Prufrock's frightened legs. She jumped this way, then that, and suddenly, she felt something thick and cold fall on her back.

Fear! Prufrock felt fear, thick and cold, and it was like nothing she had felt before in her young life. She felt her small body grow stiff with terror, her legs shook so hard they could not hold her up.

Thwack! She jumped as the broom handle hit the floor, missing her by inches. The floor felt uncertain and slippery under her frightened legs. They scrabbled for footing, and just as the broom handle came down again, Prufrock raced across the room to her mouse-hole and inside it, her heart hammering in her little chest. She could still feel her fear, thick and cold, sitting upon her back.

Back in her mouse-hole, her mother comforted her: 'There, there, little Pru, you're safe now,' she said. 'It's only a large drop of purple paint, and now I've got it off!'

But from that day on, Prufrock always turned purple when she was scared. Like the drop of paint that had once fallen on her back. And now, she was always scared and could not remember ever being anything but.

*

When Wisha stepped out of her Solitude Room, the Bookworm was waiting outside. 'Ah, so you have the beginning of a story, Wisha,' he said, stepping back to look at her from top to bottom. 'That's an interesting pattern.'

The Bookworm was referring to the dress Wisha was wearing. It was purple, with a mouse patch stitched neatly in the middle. There was a broom embroidered on the sleeve, two paintbrushes near the hem, a mousetrap near the neckline, a jar of purple paint caught up in the folds, and a pair of human legs that ran across the belt unannounced.

'What's this?' Wisha asked, looking down at herself in alarm. Prufrock, her mother, the artist, they were all gone but for the patches upon her dress.

'It's your Story, you tell me,' said the Bookworm.

'This is *my* Story?' asked Wisha, running the fabric of her dress between her fingers.

'It is a little lacking in Style,' said the Bookworm, circling Wisha and looking at her dress from all sides. 'It doesn't fall well, it hangs loose over your shoulders, the hem drags upon the floor, the belt needs some tightening, but it will take shape in the end.'

Wisha stood in front of her mirror and groaned.

'It doesn't even look like a dress,' she said, turning up her nose at the Roman toga she saw herself in.

'Sure it does,' said the Bookworm, laughing. 'Good writers are always too critical of their work. Too much criticism too early is not a good thing.'

With that, the Bookworm fished a pair of silver scissors out of his pocket. 'Wisha Wozzariter, meet Scissors of Style,' said the Bookworm.

The scissors bowed. Wisha bowed back. She had seen too much now to be overly surprised.

'Let me run you through the style catalogue, Wisha,' said Scissors. 'Now if you turn to the mirror, I'll show you what Style can do.'

*

What Style Can Do for You

As Wisha stared into the mirror goggle-eyed, Scissors of Style went about its work briskly, snipping a corner here, pinning up a hemline there,

and pausing every now and then to stand in front of the mirror and admire its own work.

Wisha's dress had been shortened up to her knees and one-half of it had been fashioned into a cloak that hung upon her shoulders like a dark blanket.

'There's something that this cloak is hiding from us,' said Scissors, dropping its voice to a conspiratorial whisper. 'We must find what it is before time runs out for us.'

It took Wisha a little time to comprehend, but then she rummaged inside her cloak to find what Scissors was looking for—and whipped out a dagger.

'Is this what we're looking for, Scissors, a cloak-and-dagger style?' she asked, giggling.

Scissors looked a little disappointed. 'Are you laughing? Doesn't cloak-and-dagger work for you?'

'Oh, please don't feel so bad about it,' said Wisha, trying to soften the blow. 'It's really not me, that's all.'

'Perhaps,' said Scissors, 'we could make it more frightening for you, then? Like a medieval horror?'

Before Wisha could protest, the cloak clapped itself tight over her face like a hood. Wisha's chest tightened; she felt she was in a dungeon. All around her she could hear the screams of prisoners and the clanking of rusted iron chains. She tried to scream—

'No, no terror for me either!'—but her breath felt as hot as a dragon's, singeing her cheeks.

It stopped as suddenly as it had started, the cloak growing as light as a spider's web. Before her eyes, it began flapping like a butterfly and flew away.

'Romance!' clacked the scissors. 'That must be you for sure. Butterflies, roses, springtime . . . ah!'

But romance wasn't Wisha, and neither was fantasy or sci-fi.

'No?' cried Scissors. 'None of these?'

And then Wisha's dress grew long sleeves, and those sleeves wrapped themselves around her waist and started tickling her. 'Comedy!' cried Scissors, exasperated. 'Or don't you like laughing, too?'

But Wisha wasn't looking for Comedy. Or the Whodunit. Or Poetry. Or Melodrama. Or Drama.

'Most writers are happy with the way these things fit,' said Scissors. 'What am I going to do with you?'

Wisha looked dismayed. She had a book to write and no style to call her own. What was it she wanted to be—funny, emotional, frightening, terrifying, morbid, sentimental, none of these . . . or all of these?

'A tape,' said Wisha. 'What I need is a measuring tape.'

'A measuring tape!' scoffed Scissors. 'I've already sized you up.'

'Perhaps you don't know me well enough to size me up,' retorted Wisha. 'Only I can measure my own life. Tape, please.'

Wisha used the tape to measure all her experiences. She found humour (6 ⅞ × 4 ¼ inches), fear (8 × 5 ¼ inches), sorrow (8 ¾ × 5 ⅝ inches), love (5 × 7 ½ inches). She found a good amount of self-doubt (11 × 8 ¼ inches), but the Bookworm reassured her that for writers, self-doubt went with the territory.

Together, Scissors and Wisha cut out a dress in these measurements. When Wisha put it on, it fit perfectly. They stood before the mirror—Wisha, the Bookworm and Scissors—and looked at a writer for whom no style in the world would do—but her own.

*

The Villain of the Piece

'Looking for something?' asked the Bookworm, all innocence.

Wisha had been locked inside the Solitude Room for hours. Now she was peering inside the Imagination Balloon and sighing.

Prufrock was a lot less scared of the Bookworm now. Instead of hiding inside Wisha's clothes, she reclined near the door, swishing her long tail and yawning.

'I'm here, but she doesn't know what to do with me,' said Prufrock. 'Her story just won't move forward!'

'That bad?' said the Bookworm. 'Hmmmm! What you need is a Villain and a Conflict.'

Wisha put her hands on her hips and glared at him. 'Villains give me the creeps, and I don't want any Conflict, please.'

'I didn't say you want it, I said you need it,' chuckled the Bookworm, flying out the door and slamming it shut behind him.

Wisha flung her pen at the door. 'Thanks for nothing!' she cried, when a sudden hush fell about the room. It had always been dark and silent in here, but this was different. It felt as if everything in the room were waiting for something to happen.

Then, there was a loud burst of noise—voices! It was like many people were talking, all at the same time:

Maybe it should go this way!
Maybe it should go that way!
It should take a turn for the better!
Or for the worse!

What were these voices saying? *What* should go this way or that?

There was suddenly a rush of air in the room, and the darkness was broken by flashes of light. On. Off. On. Off.

'Prufrock, are you here?' said Wisha into the darkness, her voice quavering. 'Where are we?'

As if in reply, Wisha felt the mouse move under her clothes. Except for frightened little Prufrock hiding inside her shirt, Wisha was all alone. And then there were the voices, speaking one after the other, speaking without stopping.

And now, a loud blast of sound! Was it the whistle of a train?

'I'm on the Thought Express,' said Wisha to herself. 'How very strange and sudden! And where is it taking me?'

As if in response to her last question, the train started slowing down. There was a window where the door of the Solitude Room had once stood. Wisha looked out. They were approaching a station now. It was dimly lit, so dimly lit that Wisha could barely discern the name of the station.

Where Are You Going? it said.

Where Are You Going? What sort of name was that for a station?

I don't know where I'm going, thought Wisha, and as if in response, the train started speeding up again.

It raced upon its dark tracks, and the voices on the train were all whispering together now: *Where are you going, Wisha? Where are you going?*

The train slowed down again. Another station. As dimly lit as the first. Wisha peered out once more, hoping the train would stop and let her off here. What was that? The station name—what was it?

What Happens Next?

Again, a peculiar name for a train station but Wisha gathered what this was all about. It was as if the Thought Express was asking her something.

The voices pressed closer around her now: *Yes, tell us, Wisha, what happens next? Tell us, Wisha, tell us.*

It was all too much to take in. The Thought Express was asking Wisha to think about the plot of her story. If she couldn't decide what happened next, would she ever get off the Thought Express?

Just then, the train slowed down yet again and Wisha peered out. Not another station with a question for a name, Wisha hoped.

No, there was no station here. The train had in fact stopped in darkness, in the middle of nowhere.

Now what?

Wisha leaned out of the window, craning her neck to see what was stopping the train.

It was preposterous! Up in front, an enormous black block glowed on the tracks, as if it were lit up from the inside. Who had thought to leave it there? And written on it, in lettering that sparkled, was 'Writer's Block—No Road Ahead'.

If Wisha didn't think of a way out of here soon, she would be stuck. In the middle of nowhere. Perhaps even forever. Where was the Bookworm when she needed him most?

'You have to face me alone,' said a voice, soft and menacing.

Wisha whirled around, sudden fear gripping her. She knew that rasping voice. She would know it anywhere.

Standing in the shadows, near the doorway of the train, was a stocky man in a black velveteen coat. His back was to her, but she recognized the coat.

Sikes! It was the man from the Bargain Bazaar, the man Mr Frugal had warned her about. His right arm was raised up in the air, and his fingers were wrapped about a small piece of paper.

Wisha gasped when she saw what it was! She thrust her fingers into her pocket, but it was empty.

'The Golden Scratch Card for Luck!' she said. 'That's mine, how did you get it?'

Sikes laughed a Villain's laugh, his back still turned to her. 'Picked it neat out of your pocket while you were trying to figure out What Happens Next.'

'Give it back!' cried Wisha, her cheeks growing flushed with anger.

Sikes laughed a most hideous laugh. Wisha wished he wouldn't laugh like that.

'Will you face me?' he asked her.

Wisha flew at him, but he whipped himself around.

'Easy, Wisha, easy!' he said, wielding his pen wickedly.

With a speed that surprised even her, Wisha leapt out of his way. 'Will we be fighting with pens?' she asked, half-laughing.

'Why, the pen is mightier than the sword, of course!' said Sikes, swinging his pen from side to side.

As Wisha dodged him, she spotted her own pen, the one she had thrown at the Bookworm as he left the Solitude Room. It had rolled near a wall after hitting the door. With an angry cry, she reached for it.

'There!' she said, driving him back with her pen. 'Why do you need the Scratch Card so badly?'

'I'm a Lazy Writer,' said Sikes, his voice gravelly, 'the sort who relies on Luck more than other writers do.'

As he spoke, he stepped backwards off the train, his body half-hidden in the darkness. He waved the ticket in front of her eyes.

'First I'll laugh my Villain's laugh,' he cackled. 'And then I will take your leave, Wisha. Thanks for the Scratch Card!'

Wisha was horrified. If she allowed Sikes to step off the train, she would never see her Scratch Card again.

'I'm not finished with you,' she shouted as she jumped off the train behind him.

On the train, it had been dim and shadowy, but off the train, Wisha was completely in darkness. Her ears were alert, though, and she could hear Sikes' pen making sharp cutting noises as it sliced through the air.

It was too dark to clearly see which way she was going, but Wisha backed up, away from the sound of Sikes' pen. And then she could not back up any farther! There, looming behind her, was the Writer's Block. She could feel it with her hands.

Sikes' pen sliced through the air again. She could hear him laughing into her face now, but she could not see him. He would hurt her if she didn't move away. Fast.

She pitted her entire weight against the Writer's Block, knowing in her heart that it was no use. She would never be able to move something that size.

But she was wrong. The Writer's Block was as light as papiér-mâché, and it went spinning off the tracks as she set her weight against it. The lights on the train came on, and the train started moving again.

'Of course!' said Wisha, jumping out of its path. 'I can see clearly. Now perhaps I will know What Happens Next!'

But writers don't always know what happens next. Just like Wisha didn't know that Prufrock would bite Sikes. Which she did. And hard.

His laugh was cut short by a loud shriek of pain. 'Eeeeyoowweeeee!' screamed Sikes, hopping on one leg, his arms flailing.

'Leave him there in the dark!' cried Prufrock, jumping back on the moving train. 'Get in!'

But Wisha's eyes were on her pen. Spinning.

Spinning. It had fallen out of her hands and now it would disappear into the darkness with Sikes if she got on the train without it.

'There goes your Confidence!' said Sikes, pointing to her pen and laughing his last laugh.

'You mean this, don't you?' cried Wisha, diving for her pen and pulling it into the train with her in the nick of time.

'Or this?' tittered Prufrock, the Golden Scratch Card between her teeth. 'Were you too busy laughing to notice that this was gone?' she jeered.

Sikes wasn't laughing any more. In fact, he wasn't saying anything. He was too busy limping after the train before he was swallowed up by the darkness around him. With one last dismal cry, he was gone.

The train picked up speed as it pulled away, letting out a long triumphant blast.

Wisha threw her arms around Prufrock, jumping up and down with joy. She hugged the pen and the Scratch Card close.

'Who would have thought you were so brave, Prufrock!' she cried happily.

'I didn't go looking for my courage,' beamed Prufrock, 'but I guess it found me!'

*

The Circus of Bad Form

'We need to make one more trip on the Thought Express,' said the Bookworm, popping his head into the Solitude Room.

'Why?' asked Wisha, taking her Observation Glasses off. 'An Idea, a Hero, a Villain and my own Style, don't I have everything?'

'Everything and nothing are like two sides of the same coin, aren't they?' said the Bookworm. 'Those who think they have Nothing might have Everything. And those who think they have Everything might have Nothing.'

Wisha frowned. 'You're talking funny again, Bookworm. Do I have Nothing?'

'You have Something,' said the Bookworm. 'Or, should I say, Some Things. And that's what they'll remain if you don't get yourself a tube of Structure Glue to hold them all together.'

'Enough said,' smiled Wisha. 'I feel a Thought coming on. Shall we ride on it?'

'Why not?' said the Bookworm as the Thought Express pulled in.

It was sheer craziness where the Bookworm and Wisha got off. The crowds on the platform surged like a giant wave, pushing them first one way, then another.

'Stay close,' cautioned the Bookworm. 'And if we get separated, meet me at the Big Top.'

Wisha craned her neck, looking over the heads of at least a hundred people to spot the Big Top, a red-and-white striped circus tent rising up in the distance. From where she stood, it looked enormous, ringed by gold and silver flags that fluttered in the breeze.

'Where are we?' she shouted over the din.

'At the Circus of Bad Form,' the Bookworm shouted back.

Wisha felt the ribbon in her hair come loose as they jostled with the crowd, but there was no way to turn back and retrieve it. Breathless, the Bookworm and Wisha made their way to the Big Top. It looked even larger from up close.

'What is this place?' whispered Wisha, awestruck.

'It's a freak show of every story in the world that's

been badly written,' said the Bookworm. 'The Circus of Bad Form, don't you get it?'

Wisha looked puzzled. 'And *this* is where we find our Structure Glue?'

The Bookworm nodded. 'But of course! First you need to see what happens to Stories that don't have Structure.'

Wisha broke into a smile. 'Ah, so that I appreciate Structure when I have it?'

'Sure,' said the Bookworm. 'We already have enough things that we don't appreciate. Who needs more of those?'

Inside the tent, it was hot and dank. 'Bet you can't do this!' shouted a clown, pointing at a man swallowing a long sword and a woman eating fire.

'Bah! Look at those stunts!' said the Bookworm. 'Those are the Stories with too much Show, too little Substance. Don't get taken in, move on!'

'The Largest Man in the World! Don't Miss This!' said a black sign with red lettering. A giant of a man sat on a stool that looked as small as a mushroom under him. His clothes were so tight, the buttons of his yellow jacket kept popping open. His blue pants were splitting at the seams. Words were spilling out of him in a mad garble.

'Behold the Bulky Story, written by a writer who loves the sound of his own voice,' said the Bookworm. 'Too many words, what a waste!' Bookworm wrinkled his nose at the thought.

'See the Thinnest Man next!' a loudspeaker blared over their heads, making Wisha jump.

Wisha and the Bookworm sidestepped a cartwheeling clown and a pair of circus elephants to reach the Thinnest Man. He was so lean his ribs stuck out of his chest. His elbows and knees were pointed knobs of bone.

'Recognize this one?' asked the Bookworm.

'The Skeletal Story?' guessed Wisha. 'The one the writer didn't bother to give any flesh to?'

The Bookworm looked pleased. 'Bingo!' he said. 'Now keep your eyes peeled for the tube of Structure Glue, it could be anywhere.'

A Contortionist was twisting his long arms and legs into an impossible knot. 'I know this one,' said Wisha, clapping her hands. 'A story with no bones at all! It's a twisted mess, isn't it?'

'And that's a . . .' and Wisha broke off to stare at a bearded man in a large hat crossing their path. It was odd, but his hands and feet kept falling off. '. . . A Story with Loose Ends, that's great!'

The Bookworm laughed. 'I knew you would enjoy this! Can you guess what that one is?'

Wisha peered ahead and shook her head. There were two women joined at the hip. They might have looked identical, except that one was beautiful, exquisite really, and the other, quite clearly her sister, looked deformed.

'Conjoined twins,' said the Bookworm, shrugging. 'A Good Story with a Bad Sequel.'

It was all too much to take in. Wisha looked around but she couldn't spot the tube of Structure Glue anywhere. Then, a gasp went up from the crowd. Someone at the back was screaming in excitement.

'Look!' they all said, pointing. 'Look!'

Everyone looked. What they were looking at was so high up they had to crane their necks to see it. It was a beautiful girl in a pink ballerina tutu, swinging from a trapeze high above the ground. As the crowd watched, the girl pushed her legs out, swinging the trapeze back and forth, back and forth, each time a little higher than before. Now the trapeze was flying across the roof of the circus, and the girl seemed to enjoy it, her long hair streaming behind her. She looked down at the crowd and smiled before leaning over, as though she wished to fall right off. Then, suddenly, her back arched, her hands reaching out, she threw herself forward, and now she was in the air. For a split second, she was caught there, motionless, and then just as it seemed that she would come crashing to the ground, she leapt gracefully from the first trapeze to a second one. Her fingers curled around the bar of the second trapeze, the crowd gasped, and she vaulted her body upward till she was swinging from the second trapeze, as easily as a girl on a playground might do.

'Look!' someone whispered. Wisha looked again. Could it—no, it couldn't—yes, but it was!

The trapeze artist was holding something between her teeth! She gripped the Bookworm hard. 'The tube!

I see it!' she cried. 'She has the tube of Structure Glue in her mouth, doesn't she?

'So she does!' said the Bookworm. 'Only a writer with Structure Glue can show such perfect form, such perfect timing.'

'How do we get it?' asked Wisha, all excited.

'Now that you've spotted it, the trapeze artist will throw it to you,' said the Bookworm. 'Be prepared to catch it!'

And sure enough, just at that moment, the girl looked at Wisha and winked. With a slight twist of the girl's hand, the tube went flying over the crowd, falling neatly into Wisha's outstretched hands.

'Let's go,' said the Bookworm. 'Now you have Everything, well, almost!'

'Now I have a Beginning, a Middle and an End!' said Wisha, beaming.

'That's more than I have,' said the Bookworm glumly. 'I look the same all through!'

*

The Truth Sandwich

'All good things come to an End,' pronounced the Bookworm solemnly.

'It feels like we've just begun,' said Wisha, a little sad. 'Are we There already?'

'Not yet,' said the Bookworm. 'But we can't stay Here forever. Now grab your bicycle and we'll get There together.'

Wisha shook her head in confusion. 'What bicycle?'

The Bookworm rolled his eyes. 'The one in the Imagination Balloon? The one you put in there yourself! What will you be forgetting next—Prufrock?'

Prufrock! Wisha hadn't thought that she might be coming along on this trip.

'Hop on the back of my bike, Prufrock!' Wisha said as the Bookworm clambered on to the handlebars. Then they were off.

The path was mostly uphill and Wisha had to pedal furiously just to keep her balance.

'Won't the Thought Express take us There?' she asked Wisha.

'Writers have to spend some of their time thinking, and the rest of their time doing,' said the Bookworm mysteriously. 'Time for doing, Wisha!'

'This isn't easy,' she sighed, pedalling harder. 'A car might have been an easier option on these mountain roads.'

'You thought up the bicycle and stuck it in your Imagination Balloon,' smiled the Bookworm, looking

quite comfortable curled around the bicycle bell. 'I only considered taking it along.'

Wisha grunted in reply.

The Bookworm started singing:

We've got Imagination, we've found our Style,
We have a Hero, though that took us a while,
We took the Thought Express, it was quite a ride,
We fought a Villain and Luck was on our side,
We know what happens next, Wisha, aren't we set?
Pedal on, we'll make a Writer of you yet.

He shouted the last line out loud.

'Pipe down!' ordered Wisha, panting for breath. 'This is torture!'

'Ah, but this isn't torture, it's Effort,' said the Bookworm, quite enjoying himself. 'You can't become a great writer without it.'

'When do we stop?' wheezed Wisha.

'Now, but only to let Prufrock off,' said the Bookworm. 'Goodbye, Prufrock!'

'What!' said Wisha, putting her feet on the ground and bringing the bicycle to a stop. 'Where is Prufrock going?'

'Away,' said Prufrock, jumping off.

'But you're my Hero,' said Wisha.

'Am I?' said Prufrock, climbing up Wisha's leg and settling in the crook of her arm. 'You know better, don't you?'

Wisha fell silent for a moment. Prufrock tickled Wisha's cheek with her nose. 'I'll miss you, too, Wisha,' she said. 'I wouldn't have met my courage if I hadn't met you.'

She was grey now, and she looked like any other mouse anywhere. Yet, to Wisha, she was special. Purple or not.

'B-but,' Wisha stuttered, finding her voice. 'I want you to stay.'

Prufrock sniffed at Wisha's feet with affection. 'Of course you do, but you can't tell me what to do, remember? You didn't tell me to bite Sikes, but I did, didn't I?'

Wisha nodded. 'You saved my life, Prufrock.'

Prufrock gave Wisha one last gentle nibble on her toes. 'Goodbye, Wisha,' she said. 'I feel brave to go see the world now. I'll send you a postcard from every place I visit!'

With that, Prufrock was gone.

'Gone, just like that,' said Wisha glumly as she climbed back on her bike. 'I'll miss her.'

'I'm sure you will, but you've outgrown her,' said

the Bookworm. 'You give up old stories and characters for new ones. I've seen it happen often enough.'

They rode on in thoughtful silence. Thankfully, there was no more singing from the Bookworm. It was quite peaceful, the sound of the bicycle wheels as they rolled over the road, the breeze blowing softly and a bird calling somewhere.

The Bookworm spoke at last. 'There! We're Here!'

The Bookworm was always full of surprises, so of course this was no different. Wisha had expected There to be someplace meaningful, but now that they were Here, the road ended. Like a full stop. There was nothing farther.

They had cycled up to the very top of the mountain. On the opposite side, a mighty waterfall leapt over the mountain edge and plunged downward. Wisha summoned up the courage to look down. It was a precipitous drop. She could not see the bottom of it.

'You'll need this,' said the Bookworm at last, handing Wisha a set of metal keys. It took her only the briefest moment to recall that these were the same metal keys that she had breathed into the Imagination Balloon.

'Now what?' she cried, over the loud sound of rushing water.

'I don't know,' said the Bookworm, shrugging.

Wisha's forehead creased. 'What do you mean, you don't know? You've brought me out here in the middle of nowhere, what do I do now?'

'You're the writer, you get to decide The End,' said the Bookworm calmly. 'But I have a book to get back to.'

'You can't leave me here on my own,' said Wisha.

'I just did,' said the Bookworm, and he was gone.

Wisha sat down at the very top of the mountain and watched the birds wheeling up in the sky. She dropped a stone over the mountain edge and watched it vanish. She gazed at the spray rising up from the waterfall. To have come all this way for nothing, she thought bitterly.

And then she giggled as she remembered how the boy on New Idea Street had emptied a bucket of water on her. And she shook her head over the thought of the little girl in the Superhero Salon who said her fairy wasn't pretty enough. She smiled as she recalled collecting her first drop of Inspiration. She shuddered as she thought of Sikes, howling away in the darkness as the Thought Express pulled away.

I haven't ended up the same place I've started, thought Wisha. I'm someplace different. And I'm different. This road can't go nowhere.

Nowhere.

Some familiar words came back to her like the scent of old leaves floating on a forest breeze.

A writer can be the best writer in the world, but without a stroke of Luck, he'll go nowhere.

Mr Frugal's words! The Golden Scratch Card! Where was her Luck when she needed it most?

She put her hand into the pocket of her shorts. It was empty! For one heart-stopping moment, she feared the worst. Had she dropped the Golden Scratch Card?

But then she felt a paper rustling in the other pocket. She reached inside. Her fingers closed around the torn Golden Scratch Card. Silver lettering emerged as she scratched the golden rectangle on the back.

It said:

One stroke of luck to you.

Wisha stared down at the mountain dropping away beneath her. She could turn back now. Or she could do—what? Jump?

Just then, the sunlight caught on the Golden Scratch Card, making it glow like the colours of a rainbow. Wisha looked up. A rainbow! There it was, arcing across the sky and disappearing into the water. No! Not disappearing into the water, but touching the rocks near the waterfall, almost all the way down.

'Perhaps I'll find a pot of gold at the end of this rainbow,' said Wisha, not stopping to think any longer. She clambered down the slippery rocks, praying that her Luck would show her the way.

The descent was a dangerous one, the sharp rocks glistening wet, and often too shaky to get a foothold on. She scraped her hands and feet, but she kept descending. Wisha tried not to look below her at how far she would fall if she forgot for one moment how high up she was.

And then something glimmered and it caught her eye. There, nestled in between two outcrops of rock. Right where the rainbow ended. Her pot of gold was a tiny treasure chest, golden. With shaking hands, Wisha reached out for it.

The keys the Bookworm had given her were a perfect fit and the lid swung open.

'There you are!' said the Bookworm, curled up inside the box on the daintiest little sandwich Wisha had ever seen. 'What took you so long to get here?'

'Never mind,' said Wisha, trying not to look too surprised. 'Is this lunch? It is most odd that my midday meal should come so securely packaged.'

'Go on, bite into it,' said the Bookworm. 'It's a Truth Sandwich.'

'I'm famished,' said Wisha, laughing. 'It will take a lot more than this to fill me up.'

'Eat it,' urged the Bookworm. 'You'll be surprised how satisfying the Truth can be.'

'How does it taste?' asked Wisha, holding the sandwich to her nose and taking a whiff.

'It's a little bitter,' said the Bookworm. 'But it wouldn't be the Truth if it wasn't.'

Wisha knew better than to doubt the Bookworm or question him further. Without further ado, she bit into the sandwich. It had many layers, and she could taste them all. The grittiness of the bread, the creaminess of the filling, the bitterness of the seasoning. A little crunchy, a little sour, slightly sweet. And a little inexplicable.

It didn't taste good or bad. It tasted like what it was. The Truth. Plain and simple.

How Things End

That's how it is with things. They always work out in The End.

Wisha's Golden Scratch Card helped her to find the Truth. And what was that Truth? Simply this: Wisha had a story inside her and it was a story waiting to be told.

And once Wisha realized the Truth and found her way to the End of her story, the Inspiration Bottle brimmed over. The auctioneer got more than the half-bottle promised to him.

Mr Frugal rebuilt his Thrift Shop. And he promised Wisha a wider choice of heroes for her next book.

Prufrock did a grand tour of Europe and sent Wisha a postcard from every place she visited. Her last one was from Pontikonisi, a tiny Greek island hemmed in by blue water.

It read:

My Dear Wisha,
Pontikonisi means
'Mouse Island.' Who
would have thought
they would name an
island after a mouse?
Had to sail out and see
it for myself.
Love from Greece,
Pru!

TO:
Wisha Wozzariter

So Wisha wrote her story. This story. The story of how she became a writer. A story about Wisha's adventures on the Thought Express and all the strange places it took her to, from the crowded bylanes of the Marketplace of Ideas to the slushy alleys of the Bargain Bazaar. A story about all the people she met along the way: frightened Prufrock who found her courage; shifty Sikes who would do anything for a stroke of Luck; and especially the Bookworm. A story about how Wisha learnt to use her Imagination and found her Style. But in The End, a story about how Wisha stopped wishing and started writing.

*

And what of the Bookworm? The last time Wisha saw him, he was in her book. On page 77. And he looked pleased.

*